Vedantonomics

OrangeBooks Publication

1st Floor, Rajhans Arcade, Mall Road, Kohka, Bhilai, Chhattisgarh 490020
Website: **www.orangebooks.in**

First Edition, 2025

ISBN: 978-93-6554-337-7

Price: Rs. 299.00

Printed in India

VEDANTONOMICS

A DIALOGUE BETWEEN CONSCIOUSNESS AND CAPITAL

AMIT CHATURVEDI

OrangeBooks Publication
www.orangebooks.in

To my parents…

…for nurturing me with a rare blend of modern intellect and timeless Vedic light.

To my Guru…

…the silent force behind every insight, who cleared paths I did not know were blocked.

To every teacher…

…who shaped the questions I now dare to ask.

To my sister…

…my first reader, my sharpest critic.

To my wife…

…whose steady belief remained constant through every phase of this journey.

To my two little daughters…

…whose innocent smiles turned even the densest economics into poetry.

And to God, my Eternal Guide - Shri Krishna…

…for whispering these thoughts into my heart so that I could humbly copy-paste them in this book under my own name.

Sarvopanishado gavo, dogdha gopala-nandanah

partho vatsah su-dhir bhokta, dugdham gitamritam mahat.

(Bhagavad Gita Mahatmya, Verse-6)

The Upanishads are the cow, Lord Krishna the divine milker, Arjuna the calf. The Gita is the milk, pure wisdom, and the blessed seekers are those who drink its nectar.

Acknowledgement

This book, while fictional in form, draws inspiration from some of the most timeless traditions of thought, both from classical economics and the eternal truths of Sanatana Dharma.

I wish to express my heartfelt gratitude to the many ancient rishis, sages, and thinkers whose wisdom has been preserved through scriptures such as the Bhagavad Gita, the Upanishads, Rig Veda, Manu smriti, Mahabharata, Arthashastra, and many others. The scriptural references and philosophical insights presented throughout this work are drawn from sources in the public domain. Where necessary, I have respectfully paraphrased, interpreted, or reworded verses to serve the purpose of contemporary dialogue and spiritual reflection. These adaptations are made with deep reverence and are not intended to replace traditional commentaries or scholarly translations.

I also acknowledge the contributions of countless economists, educators, and thinkers whose ideas helped shape the modern economic frameworks referenced in this work. While this book explores these concepts through a fictional dialogue, it is not meant to criticize or diminish any ideology, institution, or school of thought, either modern or ancient. Rather, it is a humble attempt to explore new intersections between value and values, between profit and purpose.

Any resemblance in characters or settings to real individuals or institutions is entirely coincidental. This work is a creative bridge, not a doctrinal statement.

If any expression within these pages has unintentionally misrepresented or hurt the sentiments of any reader, I offer my sincere apologies. The sole intent of this effort is to foster inquiry, harmony, and deeper understanding, never division.

Readers are encouraged to approach the material with a spirit of open-minded exploration, and not as doctrinal truth. Interpretations offered herein are personal and creative, and do not claim to represent any particular Parampara (spiritual lineage), economic institution, or intellectual authority.

To all readers, thinkers, seekers, and teachers, thank you for walking alongside me on this journey. May our shared pursuit of truth continue with courage, curiosity, and compassion.

Vedantonomics.online.

Preface

Throughout the course of human progress, few fields have influenced the world as deeply and as paradoxically as economics. Its theories are embedded in every nation's policy, every corporation's strategy, and every individual's dreams. Yet, with all its graphs and models, economics seems unable to answer the most fundamental questions of our time:

- Why does inequality persist despite economic growth?
- Why do wars thrive while peace is preached?
- Why are prosperous societies riddled with mental unrest, ecological degradation, and moral decay?

It was in pursuit of these questions that this book was born.

What followed was not a straight answer, but a conversation. A fictional dialogue between a curious student and a professor who speaks in both GDP and Gita, spreadsheets and shlokas.

Vedantonomics is not merely a play of words, it is a revolution in thinking. It is the confluence of two mighty rivers: the empirical sharpness of economics and the eternal depth of Vedanta. While one studies the mechanics of human choices, the other reveals the wisdom behind them. While one seeks to maximize utility, the other strives for Moksha (Liberation).

This book unfolds as a dialogue between two characters, Bharat, an inquisitive economics student frustrated with the limitations of modern theories, and Professor Madhav, a well-known economist and scholar of Vedic philosophy. Through a series of vivid, humorous, and profound conversations, they explore everything from the illusion of rationality to the futility of GDP worship, from Keynes and Krugman to Krishna and Kapila.

Inspired by the timeless mentor-student spirit of the Bhagavad Gita, you may find echoes of Krishna in Professor Madhav's calm brilliance, and perhaps a shadow of Arjuna in Bharat's restless quest.

Each chapter ends with sharp comparisons between modern economic theories and their Vedic counterparts, shlokas with explanations, real-world economic failures, and policy ideas based on Dharma. The goal is not to replace economics but to elevate it, from a science of numbers to a philosophy of life.

Vedantonomics is an exploration, not a conclusion. It is my humble attempt to place the soul back into economics, not by rejecting modernity, but by realigning it with ancient wisdom. Through eleven thematic chapters, I've tried to spark a conversation between two seemingly distant worlds: the evolving graphs of global economics and the eternal truths of Sanatana Dharma.

While this book draws from real philosophies and theories, it remains a work of fiction. The characters, settings, and dialogues are intentionally crafted for narrative expression. It is not meant to critique or diminish any economic school, Vedic tradition, ideology, community, gender, or nation. Rather, it is a humble and exploratory effort to bridge the world of modern economic thought with the timeless wisdom of Sanatana Dharma. My only intention is to invite reflection, not reaction.

May this book serve as a small step toward a more conscious economy, and a more compassionate world.

As the world hurtles toward greater complexity, it is time we rediscover the simplicity of truth.

This is not just a book. It is a conversation we must have.

Welcome to Vedantonomics.

Regards,

- Amit Chaturvedi

Introduction

Rethinking Prosperity at the Crossroads of Dharma and Demand.

Economics is meant to be the study of human choice. But what if the questions we've been asking are too shallow for the human spirit?

What if rationality as defined by markets is just another name for conditioning? What if the pursuit of wealth, without wisdom, leads not to abundance but alienation? What if, beneath the curves of supply and demand, lie subtler forces, **Desire**, **Dharma**, **Karma**, and **Moksha**, that truly shape our decisions?

Welcome to Vedantonomics, a reflective, often playful, and sometimes provocative conversation between modern economics and ancient wisdom. It is a journey to explore how Vedantic philosophy, the spiritual heart of India's Vedic tradition, can enrich our understanding of human motivation, societal wellbeing, and the purpose of prosperity.

Rethinking Economics: From Crisis to Consciousness

Modern economics, rooted in Enlightenment thinking, views humans as rational, self-interested agents **Homo Economicus** and markets as efficient allocators. While this model has fuelled material progress, it has also triggered:

- Environmental degradation
- Deepening inequality
- Widespread dissatisfaction, even amid affluence

GDP has risen, but so have burnout, loneliness, and spiritual void.

Vedanta: A Deeper Lens

Vedanta, the spiritual core of the Vedas, sees humans not as consumers, but as **conscious beings (Atman)** pursuing four life goals (**Purusharthas**): Dharma (duty), Artha (wealth), Kama (desire), and Moksha (liberation). These are not in conflict but must flow in harmony - wealth and desire anchored in Dharma and aimed toward inner fulfilment.

From Homo Economicus to Homo Spiritualis

Vedantonomics offers a shift: from maximizing consumption to realizing purpose. It reimagines:

- **Wealth** as service
- **Desire** as refined, not endless
- **Work** as sacred offering (Yajna)
- **Policy** as Dharma-aligned, not just efficient

True prosperity, it argues, lies in conscious choices, ethical systems, and inner well-being, not just in output, but in outcomes that elevate the soul.

What This Book Is, and Is Not

This book is not a rejection of capitalism or socialism. Nor is it a spiritual sermon dressed up in economic terms. Rather, it is a dialogue, a narrative-driven reflection between two characters, Bharat and Professor Madhav, representing the restless seeker and the contemplative guide.

Vedantonomics is not just a blend of philosophies. It is a living dialogue, a modern *Upanishad*, between an earnest student and a professor who speaks the language of balance sheets and Bhagavad Gita with equal ease.

Set in the vibrant world of campus cafés and banyan-tree debates, this book unravels eleven major economic ideas, from rationality and competition to governance and ideology, and places them in deep conversation with India's timeless spiritual traditions.

The characters, conversations, and scenarios are dramatized for narrative impact. While based on real philosophical and economic ideas, the book does not claim to represent any single school or scripture definitively. Rather, it is a novice attempt to bridge two knowledge systems, modern economic reasoning and Sanātana Dharma, so they may enrich, question, and inform one another.

Why Vedantonomics, Why Now?

In a world facing climate crisis, inequality, and spiritual fatigue, the time is ripe for a new economic lens - one that honours complexity, promotes compassion, and balances material needs with inner peace. Vedantonomics is an offering in that direction, a humble attempt to reframe prosperity not as excess, but as enough; not as conquest, but as consciousness.

So, if you've ever felt that something's missing in the textbook graphs, if you've questioned the utility of utility functions, or if you're curious whether GDP can ever measure grace, this book is for you.

Welcome to Vedantonomics, where Dharma meets demand, supply bows to sacrifice, value means far more than price and the economy finally remembers the soul within it.

कार्पण्यदोषोपहतस्वभाव:
पृच्छामि त्वां धर्मसम्मूढचेता: |
यच्छ्रेय: स्यान्निश्चितं ब्रूहि तन्मे
शिष्यस्तेऽहं शाधि मां त्वां प्रपन्नम् ||

kārpaṇya-doṣhopahata-svabhāvaḥ
pṛichchhāmi tvāṁ dharma-sammūḍha-chetāḥ
yach-chhreyaḥ syānniśhchitaṁ brūhi tanme
śhiṣhyaste 'haṁ śhādhi māṁ tvāṁ prapannam

(Bhagavad Gita, Ch-2, Verse-7)

I stand confused about my path, overwhelmed by doubt and weakness.
As your disciple, I surrender at your feet,
guide me clearly toward what is truly right for me.

Content

1

The Irrational Rationality

If people were truly rational,
the economy would be spiritual.

Delhi University's Economics Department was a curious paradox in itself, equal parts colonial charm and contemporary chaos. Its weathered corridors echoed with the footsteps of aspiring economists, while its open courtyards hosted heated debates over policy, poverty, and the latest inflation report. Somewhere between the textbook theories and campus activism, you could always find Bharat.

Bharat was a final-year postgraduate student, sharp in mind but unsettled in spirit. He could deconstruct economic models with precision, but lately, they felt more like hollow scaffolding than structures of truth. The deeper he went into his coursework, utility curves, rational choice theory, behavioural assumptions, the more disconnected he felt from the messy, emotional world around him. He watched people make wildly irrational decisions every day, from impulse shopping to voting against their own interests, and began to wonder: Was economics a map of reality or merely a mirror of our assumptions?

Professor Madhav had recently returned to campus after a year-long sabbatical in the Himalayas. A rare blend of scholarly sharpness and spiritual depth, Madhav was often described as someone who could quote both Keynes and Krishna in the same breath. Students admired him. Colleagues misunderstood him. But no one could ignore him. His classes weren't lectures, they were philosophical provocations.

That afternoon, Bharat was nursing a lukewarm samosa at the buzzing café tucked beside the department's ivy-covered walls. His spiral notebook lay open on the table, filled with frustrated scribbles and sarcastic graphs.

Another lecture on Rational Choice Theory, he muttered, stabbing at the samosa like it had singlehandedly crashed the economy. Humans always act to maximize utility? Really? I saw a man buy bitcoin at its peak and a mango in December. What part of that screams rational?

As if on cue, a calm yet unmistakable voice broke his monologue.

You look like Keynes in 1930 after reading Hayek, said Professor Madhav, placing his tea gently on Bharat's table. What's troubling you, Bharat?

Professor, are we seriously supposed to believe people are rational? If that's true, then the world's clearly a madhouse, being run by economists.

Madhav chuckled. Rationality, in modern economics, isn't about wisdom, it's about predictability. Consistent choices to maximize some imaginary utility. But Vedanta offers a more nuanced view of why we act.

Bharat leaned forward. Please enlighten me, because I'm dangerously close to writing a thesis titled *'The Economics of Absurdity.'*

So, we assume everyone is Buddha with a spreadsheet? he added dryly.

Madhav smiled. No, we assume people are conscious beings, driven by forces subtler than numbers. The illusion of rationality is just Maya in a necktie.

Bharat blinked. You're telling me all of economics is just well-dressed delusion?

Let me put it differently, Madhav offered. Economics says people are Homo Economicus, calculating machines seeking maximum satisfaction.

Vedanta sees us as Homo Spiritualis, souls navigating existence under the influence of the three gunas:

Sattva (clarity), Rajas (desire), and Tamas (ignorance)

He pulled out a pen and sketched a quick chart on Bharat's notebook.

Compare the two models, Madhav said, as he pointed:

Concept	Economics	Vedanta
Human Nature	Homo Economicus	Homo Spiritualis
Basis of Action	Utility Maximization	Guna-Driven Karma
Knowledge	Assumes complete & perfect	Conditioned, limited, subjective
Decision Goal	Maximize Utility	Align with Dharma
Ethics	External, optional	Inherent in action (Dharma-bound)

Desires	Given and static	Conditioned by shifting Gunas

See, he said. The economic model assumes you have full knowledge and fixed preferences.

Vedanta says: no, you're being constantly swayed by your guna of the moment.

Bharat scratched his head. So, when I ordered two chocolate lava cakes last night, that wasn't irrational?

That, Madhav grinned, was Tamas at work, ignorance and indulgence. Economics would say you were maximizing utility. Vedanta would ask, *what guna influenced your utility?*

So utility is not the villain, guna is the puppet master?

Exactly. Gita 14.5 tells us:

'Material nature consists of the three gunas, goodness, passion, and ignorance. When the soul contacts nature, it becomes conditioned by these modes.'

Bharat leaned back, impressed. No wonder policy models fall apart.

Madhav nodded. Take the 2008 Financial Crisis. Economists assumed market participants acted rationally, evaluating risk, optimizing portfolios.

But instead, Bharat trailed off.

They acted out of Rajas, greed, and Tamas, delusion, Madhav finished. Packaging subprime debt as AAA securities isn't a rational act; it's a tamasic one. Without *Sattva*, society degenerates into consumption without conscience.

He added, Gita 18.38 says:

'Pleasure arising from sense contact appears like nectar but ends in poison.'

That's basically a footnote to every boom-and-bust cycle in modern finance.

Bharat whistled softly. So, what else does Rational Choice Theory ignore?

Madhav held up three fingers.

First, he said, it assumes preferences are consistent. ***But desires shift, hourly.***

Second, he added, it assumes perfect information. ***Which is laughable, even with Google.***

Third, he concluded, it ignores morality. It never asks **if the choice is right, only if it's efficient.**

Which is how we end up optimizing GDP while destroying forests, Bharat said.

Exactly. That's why Vedanta replaces utility with ***Dharma.*** Because without Dharma, Madhav paused, rationality is just decorated delusion.

Key Reflections

Bharat's Curiosity	Madhav's Wisdom
❖ Why do we assume people are rational?	❖ Because we like clean equations, not complex truths.
❖ So, what drives choice if not rationality?	❖ The Guna's: Sattva brings clarity, Rajas brings desire, Tamas brings illusion.
❖ And what corrects this?	❖ Dharma. Without Dharma, rationality is just decorated delusion.

न हि प्रपश्यामि ममापनुद्याद्
यच्छोकमुच्छोषणमिन्द्रियाणाम् ।
अवाप्य भूमावसपत्नमृद्धं
राज्यं सुराणामपि चाधिपत्यम् ॥

na hi prapaśhyāmi mamāpanudyād
yach-chhokam uchchhoṣhaṇam-indriyāṇām
avāpya bhūmāv-asapatnamṛiddhaṁ
rājyaṁ surāṇāmapi chādhipatyam
(Bhagavad Gita, Ch-2, Verse-8)

I can find no means of driving away this anguish that is drying up my senses. Even if I win a prosperous and unrivalled kingdom on the earth, or gain sovereignty like the celestial gods, I will be unable to dispel this grief.

2

The GDP Mirage: Why Growth Doesn't Mean Progress

GDP measures how fast we're running, not where we're going.

It was late afternoon. The banyan tree cast a long shadow on the university lawn as Bharat walked beside Professor Madhav.

You know what's ironic? Bharat began. GDP grows every quarter. Stock markets hit all-time highs. Yet, suicides rise, glaciers melt, and traffic jams grow longer than my patience during macroeconomics lectures.

Madhav smiled. That's because, my dear Bharat, the modern world measures fever and calls it fitness.

So, GDP is the economic thermometer of a sick civilization?

Sometimes, yes, Madhav said, sipping his chai. Tell me, what is GDP?

Gross Domestic Product. The sum of all goods and services produced in a country.

Correct, Madhav nodded. Now here's the Vedantic twist:

GDP is also the sum total of all desires acted upon, without discrimination.

Bharat raised an eyebrow.

Think about it, Madhav continued. GDP includes cigarette sales, legal battles, pollution clean-up, disaster reconstruction, and arms manufacturing. But it ignores household lab or, parenting, meditation, and spiritual growth.

So, a factory that pollutes a river contributes more to GDP than a monk who teaches values for free? Bharat asked.

Exactly, said Madhav. Because GDP sees transaction, not transformation.

Bharat looked stunned. Then it's like a drunk driver speeding toward a cliff… and economists cheer the mileage!

Madhav chuckled. GDP is agnostic to goodness. It celebrates speed, not direction.

The Gita says,

'One who is devoted to the path of selfless action attains perfection. Such a person is truly wise' (Bhagavad Gita 2.50).

Wisdom, not wealth, is the Vedantic ideal.

Bharat flipped open his notebook. Okay, let's line this up. GDP vs Vedanta, round two!

Madhav leaned in. Alright, let's reframe it.

Bharat scribbled as Madhav spoke:

GDP says:

- More production = better.
- Work is for income.
- Success is market value.
- Growth is material expansion.
- All spending is good, whether on hospitals or bombs.

Vedanta says:

- Produce only in alignment with Dharma.
- Work is duty, not just a pay check (Karma Yoga).
- True success is self-realization.
- Growth means inner evolution, not external inflation.
- Spending without purpose is like feeding a fire hoping it'll go out.

Bharat smirked. And let me guess, GDP ignores inequality, pollution, unpaid work, and mental health?

Exactly, Madhav nodded. It mistakes motion for meaning. *Progress without purpose is perilous.*

So, what are Vedantic metrics of progress? Bharat asked.

Madhav raised his fingers one by one:

- Growth in Sattva, clarity, balance, and harmony.
- Reduction in Kama, unnecessary desires.
- Alignment with Dharma, ethical living.
- Collective well-being, or Samasti.
- And ultimately, the pursuit of Moksha, liberation.

And the economy? Bharat asked.

It must be a vehicle, not a destination.

Madhav paused, then quoted:

Everything in this universe belongs to the Supreme. One should therefore accept only what is necessary, and set aside the rest (Isha Upanishad, Verse 1).

Bharat looked up. No offense, Professor, but that sounds nothing like modern development models.

True. But some are trying, Madhav said. Bhutan uses Gross National Happiness instead of GDP. They measure well-being, spiritual, ecological, cultural.

I read somewhere the 2004 tsunami boosted GDP because of all the rebuilding.

Indeed. More cement, more spending, more 'growth'. But tell me, does that reflect progress, or tragedy?

Bharat fell silent.

And during the COVID-19 pandemic, Madhav continued, pharmaceutical profits soared, while human suffering deepened. GDP grew in parts, but collective peace shrank.

Economics asks ‘how much?’ Vedanta asks, ‘for what purpose?’ Madhav said.

Bharat looked thoughtful. So, what you’re saying is the soul needs more than stimulus packages.

Exactly. A civilization without Dharma may grow economically, but it rots spiritually.

Key Reflections

Bharat's Curiosity	Madhav's Wisdom
❖ Is GDP really the best indicator of development?	❖ It's a speedometer, not a compass.
❖ Then what should we measure?	❖ Dharma, Sattva, service to others, inner peace.
❖ What's the cost of ignoring that?	❖ A society rich in numbers, poor in purpose.

न कर्मणामनारम्भान्नैष्कर्म्यं पुरुषोऽश्नुते ।
न च संन्यसनादेव सिद्धिं समधिगच्छति ॥

na karmaṇām anārambhān naiṣhkarmyaṁ puruṣho 'śhnute
na cha sannyasanād eva siddhiṁ samadhigachchhati
(Bhagavad Gita, Ch-3, Verse-4)

One cannot achieve freedom from karmic reactions by merely abstaining from work, nor can one attain perfection of knowledge by mere physical renunciation.

3

The Myth of Infinite Desires: From Demand Curves to Discipline

Desires are like fire, feed them and they blaze. Starve them and they glow within.

Bharat and Professor Madhav sat beneath their now-favorite banyan tree. A flock of students passed by, their eyes glued to smartphones and ice cream cones.

Professor, Bharat began, flipping through his notes, I just finished studying consumer behaviour theory. The curve looks beautiful, but the assumptions feel like fantasy. Infinite desires, diminishing utility... but no end to want?

Madhav smiled. Indeed, Bharat. Modern economics is built on a peculiar principle: that human wants are unlimited. So, the economy's role becomes feeding that insatiable hunger.

Sounds like trying to fill a leaky bucket.

Or worse, Madhav said, feeding a fire with butter.

Bhagavad Gita 3.39 says,

'Desire is the eternal enemy of the wise, born of the mode of passion, insatiable like fire.'

Bharat blinked. So basically, the entire demand curve is Rajas with a ruler?

Very good, Madhav laughed. In Vedanta, desires, or Kama, aren't inherently evil. But they are conditioned by the gunas. Rajas' fuels craving, Tamas clouds judgment, and only Sattva can bring contentment, Santosha.

Bharat jotted notes quickly. So, wait the economic model assumes demand rises with income. But Vedanta says desires should be restrained by Dharma?

Exactly. Vedanta teaches that desire is not a right, it's a responsibility. If unregulated, it becomes destructive. Mundaka *Upanishad* 2.2.5 says:

'The one who has realized the Self has no desires.'

The wise don't demand more, they need less.

Bharat leaned back. If desires are infinite is economics the study of managing madness?

Madhav chuckled. Not madness, just misdirected hunger. True fulfilment comes from mastering desire, not multiplying it.

Bharat grinned. So advertising is modern Rishi Kashyap, creating demons of consumption?

Madhav laughed aloud. Quite right. Every popup ad is a Rakta Beej, slay one, and a hundred more rise. The modern economy thrives on Rajas, and consumerism keeps it spinning.

Bharat scribbled in his notebook:

The Demand Curve vs. The Discipline Curve

In Economics:

- Desires are infinite.
- Demand rises with income.
- Satisfaction drops after too much (DMU - Diminishing Marginal Utility).

In Vedanta:

- Desires are products of the gunas.
- True contentment comes through Sattva (clarity).

- Dharma disciplines desire, not income.

Bharat looked up. And what happens when we let demand dictate everything?

Madhav grew serious. You get what we see today, debt-ridden youth chasing gadgets, ecological collapse from hyper-consumption, and anxiety despite abundance.

Sounds about right, Bharat sighed. I saw a friend cry over not getting the latest phone, and he had three already.

Madhav nodded. Vedanta offers a discipline-based economy. *Aparigraha*, non-hoarding, limits greed. *Santosha*, contentment, brings joy. *Yoga Sutras* 2.42 says:

'From contentment, comes supreme happiness.'

Desire isn't the villain, Madhav added softly. Attachment is. And *Bhagavad Gita* 18.38 warns us:

'That which appears like nectar at first becomes poison in the end.'

That's Rajas at work.

Bharat looked thoughtful. So, in a way, minimalism is Vedanta in skinny jeans?

Madhav smiled. Perhaps. Modern minimalism mirrors Aparigraha. Even *social media ads* aren't evil, but they manipulate the Rajas guna.

Final scribbles in Bharat's notebook:

Desire in Economics vs. Vedanta

Concept	Modern Economics	Vedic Philosophy
Nature of Desire	Infinite	Conditioned by Gunas
Function	Drives demand and growth	Must align with Dharma
Management	Income, substitution	Self-restraint, Santosha
Consequences	Overconsumption, anxiety	Liberation from craving
Ultimate Solution	Satisfy more wants	Reduce and purify wants

Bharat looked up as the sun dipped low behind the library dome. So, we assume everyone makes decisions logically and consistently?

Madhav smiled. No, Bharat. Economics assumes people are rational calculators. Vedanta sees them as conscious beings, swayed by Sattva, Rajas, and Tamas.

And economists call it demand. Vedanta calls it delusion.

Well said.

They both laughed as a nearby billboard lit up with an ad for the ***Next Big Thing***.

Key Reflections

Bharat's Curiosity	Madhav's Wisdom
❖ Why does economics assume we want everything?	❖ Because it doesn't understand the mind.
❖ Is there an economic model of contentment?	❖ Yes. It's called Santosha. It's priceless.
❖ So not all demand is desirable?	❖ Only the desire aligned with Dharma leads to peace.

न हि कश्चित्क्षणमपि जातु तिष्ठत्यकर्मकृत् ।
कार्यते ह्यवशः कर्म सर्वः प्रकृतिजैर्गुणैः ॥

na hi kaśhchit kṣhaṇam api jātu tiṣhṭhatyakarma-kṛit
kāryate hyavaśhaḥ karma sarvaḥ prakṛiti-jair guṇaiḥ
(Bhagavad Gita, Ch-3, Verse-5)

There is no one who can remain without action even for a moment. Indeed, all beings are compelled to act by their qualities born of material nature (the three guṇas).

4

Dharma Over Demand: The Ethical Backbone of True Economics

A society without Dharma is like a market without prices, chaotic, confused, and corrupt.

Bharat was unusually quiet. Not the kind of quiet that comes from a lack of coffee, but the one that comes from contemplation.

Professor, he said, I think I get it now. Desire is not inherently bad. It's the misalignment of desire that causes collapse, personal or economic.

Madhav nodded. And what ensures that alignment?

Dharma, Bharat replied.

Excellent. Now let's go deeper into that.

They continued walking along the corridor flanked by rustling neem trees. The late afternoon breeze carried the scent of rain and roasted peanuts from a distant stall.

Professor, Bharat said, in class we talk about market efficiency, taxation, fiscal multipliers but no one ever asks if the outcomes are just. We studied taxation theory without ever asking if the taxes were fair.

That's because modern economics prides itself on being value-neutral, Madhav replied. It claims to describe 'what is,' not 'what ought to be.'

So, it side lines ethics?

It strips them away in the name of objectivity, Madhav said. But Vedanta doesn't make that separation. Dharma is not an add-on, it's the foundation. It governs Artha (wealth) and Kama (desire), ensuring neither becomes destructive.

Like a riverbank for the flow of the market, Bharat suggested.

Precisely. Markets without Dharma are like rivers without banks, powerful, but prone to flood and destroy.

A billboard flickered in the distance with a slogan: Upgrade Everything. Bharat shook his head.

Even the slogans are adharmic, he muttered.

Madhav chuckled. Well spotted.

So, GDP is a thermometer, and Dharma is the immune system?

Yes, and when Dharma breaks down, economic fevers rise.

But no one talks about long-term consequences, Bharat added. It's all discounted cash flows.

Vedanta reminds us of Karmic consequences, across lives, not just quarters. The Manu smriti says,

***'Wealth earned through
Dharma brings prosperity;
wealth through Adharma leads to ruin.'***

And the Gita?

***'Perform duty without attachment.
That action leads to the Supreme.'***

They paused at a tea stall. Steam swirled from two clay cups.

So, what's the Vedantic role of a business? Bharat asked.

Business is Yajna, Madhav said, a sacrifice for the greater good, not a platform for personal greed. The goal is not profit, but Purification.

Bharat sipped thoughtfully. And yet we cheer the quarterly profits of companies that dodge taxes and exploit workers.

That's the result of mistaking legality for Dharma.

Bharat nodded. So, Dharma must become a filter for policy too, not just profit and performance.

Yes. Dharma guides not just action but intention. Without it, even economic brilliance leads to ruin. Remember, modern systems have laws. Vedantic systems have **Swadharma.**

They watched students rush by, some cramming for exams, others laughing over phone screens. A society buzzing with activity, yet often without alignment.

Professor, Bharat said, we need to teach economics as if ethics mattered.

Madhav smiled, eyes warm. Then let this be our yajna, our offering to future minds.

Key Reflections

Bharat's Curiosity	Madhav's Wisdom
❖ Where is ethics in economics?	❖ Hidden beneath equations, waiting for Dharma to awaken it.
❖ Can Dharma be taught in B-schools?	❖ Only if we teach how to live, not just how to earn.
❖ What if markets reject Dharma?	❖ Then society pays the price, slowly, painfully, inevitably.

तस्मादसक्त: सततं कार्यं कर्म समाचर |
असक्तो ह्याचरन्कर्म परमाप्नोति पूरुष: ||

tasmād asaktaḥ satataṁ kāryaṁ karma samāchara
asakto hyācharan karma param āpnoti pūruṣhaḥ
(Bhagavad Gita, Ch-3, Verse-19)

Therefore, giving up attachment, perform actions as a matter of duty because by working without being attached to the fruits, one attains the Supreme.

5

Moksha Over Market: The Ultimate Goal Beyond Consumption

If the market is the battlefield,
Moksha is the victory, not profit.

It was the kind of morning where the sun looked curious, just like Bharat.

Professor, Bharat began, every economic model stops at consumption, income, and maybe some tax optimization. But where does it all lead? What's the endgame?

Madhav smiled. In economics, the end is satisfaction. In Vedanta, the end is liberation.

So, while economists aim for maximized utility, Vedanta seeks Moksha?

Precisely. Economics says, 'fulfil your wants.' Vedanta asks, 'Who wants what, and why?'

Bharat sat down on a bench nearby. Modern life is like a treadmill, lots of motion, no direction.

And Moksha, said Madhav, is stepping off that treadmill, not by quitting life, but by waking up to its deeper meaning.

He plucked a fallen leaf. Look at this. A tree lets go when the time comes. That's Vairagya, detachment. Not out of despair, but maturity.

Bharat smiled. So real wealth is detachment, not digits in a demat account?

Exactly. Moksha is the only surplus that doesn't fluctuate with the market.

They watched a group of students across the lawn snapping selfies in front of the commerce building. Laughter, filters, and dopamine on loop.

Professor, our textbooks measure success in income, growth, assets.

And yet burnout, anxiety, and discontent are rising, Madhav said. This is what happens when we confuse the pleasant with the good.

Katha Upanishad, right? Bharat offered. The good and the pleasant come to a man. The wise choose the good.

Madhav nodded approvingly. Bhagavad Gita too:

'Supreme bliss comes to the yogi whose mind is tranquil and whose passions are quieted.'

So, we've built systems that amplify passions and call it progress.

That's because modern economics treats desire as infinite and fulfilment as external, Madhav said. Vedanta says, fulfilment is internal. Life is not about acquiring more, but desiring less.

Makes sense, Bharat said. A liberated soul must be the most productive one, not because he earns more, but because he disturbs less.

Well said, Madhav replied. And remember: Moksha is not escape. It's full engagement with life, minus bondage.

Bharat looked toward the distant city skyline. Billboards, cranes, condos.

Sometimes I wonder if all this ambition is just sophisticated craving.

Madhav smiled gently. That's why we need Jnana, discernment. To see the real from the unreal. And Nish Kama Karma, to act without clinging to the outcome.

They sat in silence for a moment. A quietness not of absence, but presence.

Bharat finally said, Professor, I think I understand. The market measures how much we can get. Moksha measures how little we need.

And that, said Madhav, is the most radical freedom of all.

Key Reflections

Bharat's Curiosity	Madhav's Wisdom
❖ What lies beyond consumption?	❖ Freedom from needing to consume.
❖ So, Moksha is economic too?	❖ It's the economics of the soul.
❖ What if society ignores Moksha?	❖ Then it becomes rich in things, but bankrupt in peace.

कर्मणैव हि संसिद्धिमास्थिता जनकादय: |
लोकसंग्रहमेवापि सम्पश्यन्कर्तुमर्हसि ||
यद्यदाचरति श्रेष्ठस्तत्तदेवेतरो जन: |
स यत्प्रमाणं कुरुते लोकस्तदनुवर्तते ||

karmaṇaiva hi sansiddhim āsthitā janakādayaḥ
loka-saṅgraham evāpi sampaśhyan kartum arhasi
yad aphasia ācharati śhreṣhṭhas tat tad evetaro janaḥ
sa yat pramāṇaṁ kurute lokas tad anuvartate
(Bhagavad Gita, Ch-3, Verse-20, 21)

By performing their prescribed duties, King Janak and others attained perfection. You should also perform your duties to set an example for the good of the world. Whatever actions great persons perform, common people follow. Whatever standards they set, all the world pursues.

6

The Real Invisible Hand: Karma as the True Regulator

Markets may be invisible, but Karma never is.

Bharat twirled his pen like a warrior spins his sword.

Professor, economists talk about the 'Invisible Hand' of the market. It sounds mystical, like economics suddenly discovered God. But sometimes, that hand seems to slap the poor and shake hands with the rich.

Madhav nodded. The Invisible Hand, as Adam Smith described, is the idea that individual self-interest unintentionally benefits society. But Vedanta teaches us of another invisible force, Karma. And unlike the market's hand, Karma doesn't miss a transaction.

Bharat smirked. So, Karma audits our balance sheet?

Continuously, Madhav replied, and across lifetimes.

Then every unethical trade is a loan with cosmic interest?

Yes, Madhav said, eyes twinkling. Karma compounds, faster than any investment portfolio.

Bharat leaned back. So, while the market values efficiency, Karma values intention.

And justice, added Madhav. Karma doesn't ask if you were rich or poor. It only asks, *were you just?*

They watched as a food delivery biker zoomed by, dodging potholes and deadlines.

You know, Bharat said, our lectures on market equilibrium made it seem like supply and demand would magically sort everything out. But reality feels… messier.

That's because the market's balance sheet ignores Dharma, Madhav said. Vedanta teaches that Karma, not price signals, is the true regulator of harmony. A society that eats alone, hoards wealth, and ignores the suffering of others accumulates collective Karma.

Rig Veda, right? Bharat recalled. The one who eats alone is a sinner. The one who feeds others first is noble.

Madhav smiled. Exactly. Markets focus on gain. Vedanta focuses on grace.

So, Karma is like long-term economic justice, but without lobbyists?

Madhav chuckled. You could say that. Modern economics assumes moral neutrality. Karma insists there's no such thing. Even thoughts and intentions matter.

Bharat grew quiet. Then maybe economics should come with a mirror, not just a calculator.

Well said, Madhav replied. In the end, the most important asset is not capital, but *consciousness*.

A gust of wind rustled the banyan leaves above them.

So, Professor, Bharat said, can a business be run with Karma in mind?

Absolutely. Through Nishkama Karma, acting without selfish attachment. Through Yajna, treating work as service. Through Seva, making selflessness structural. And through Ahimsa, doing no harm, even economically.

Bharat's brow furrowed, then brightened. Then maybe the real invisible hand isn't economics at all. It's Karma, guided by Dharma.

Madhav smiled. Now you're seeing clearly. The economy changes when the inner economy transforms.

Key Reflections

Bharat's Curiosity	Madhav's Wisdom
❖ Does the market regulate itself?	❖ Only when guided by Dharma. Otherwise, Karma takes over.
❖ So even profitable actions can be karmically toxic?	❖ Yes, especially if they harm others or nature.
❖ Then Karma is the real invisible hand?	❖ The most accurate, incorruptible one ever known.

सक्ता: कर्मण्यविद्वांसो यथा कुर्वन्ति भारत |
कुर्याद्विद्वांस्तथासक्तश्चिकीर्षुर्लोकसंग्रहम् ||

saktāḥ karmaṇyavidvānso yathā kurvanti bhārata
kuryād vidvāns tathāsaktaśh chikīrṣhur loka-saṅgraham
(Bhagavad Gita, Ch-3, Verse-25)

As ignorant people perform their duties with attachment to the results, O scion of Bharat, so should the wise act without attachment, for the sake of leading people on the right path.

7
Competition Vs Cooperation: Redefining Economic Fitness

If competition is the engine, cooperation is the soul.

Bharat was staring at a bar graph on his laptop, showing rising market shares and falling employee morale across industries.

Professor, we say competition drives innovation. But all I see is stress, burnout, and cutthroat behavior dressed up in corporate suits.

Madhav gently placed a book down and replied, When Darwin meets Davos, survival becomes a business KPI. But in Vedanta, life is not about outpacing others, it's about uplifting all.

But isn't competition healthy for progress?

Only if tempered by cooperation. The Vedas speak not of conquest, but saha-yajna, mutual sacrifice and service. Rig Veda 10.191.2 says:

'Meet together, speak together,
let your minds be of one accord.'

Progress without shared Dharma leads to progress for the few, at the cost of the many.

Bharat tilted his head thoughtfully. So, Vedanta doesn't reject excellence, but it questions isolation?

Exactly, Madhav said. Competition that forgets compassion becomes a war. Cooperation rooted in Dharma becomes culture.

Bharat laughed softly. Capitalism makes us sprint solo. Vedanta asks us to walk together.

And, Madhav smiled, the one who walks with others often reaches further.

Bharat looked back at the graph. So, in a Vedic economy, even market leaders would uplift competitors?

Yes, Madhav said firmly. Because the true measure of success is how many rises with you, not how many you leave behind.

Inspired, Bharat flipped open his notebook and began scribbling.

Let me create a table to capture this, he said.

Concept	Modern Economic View	Vedantic View
Growth Driver	Rivalry and market share	Mutual upliftment and Dharma
Motivation	Beating others	Serving others (Seva)
Impact	Winner-takes-all	Collective well-being
Social Outcome	Inequality, fragmentation	Harmony, unity (Samasti)
Ideal Firm	Disruptive innovator	Conscious contributor

Bharat paused and looked up; this makes too much sense to not be taught in B-schools.

Madhav chuckled, Now add this below your table.

Problems with Pure Competition:

- Breeds anxiety, insecurity, and aggression.
- Leads to monopolies, inequality, and exploitation.
- Encourages zero-sum thinking.
- Fosters jealousy and burnout.

Vedantic Alternatives:

- **Yajna:** Collaboration as sacred offering.
- **Sahakarita:** Shared ownership and responsibility.
- **Satsang:** Wisdom through collective learning.
- **Samatva:** Equanimity in success and failure.

Madhav added, As the Bhagavad Gita 3.10 says:

'In the beginning, the Creator created humanity along with sacrifice and said: by this shall you prosper.'

That's the blueprint we've forgotten. Bharat nodded slowly; this might be the first economic philosophy that's truly about well-being. Madhav smiled, because in Vedanta, the strongest aren't those who win alone, but those who carry others with them.

Key Reflections

Bharat's Curiosity	Madhav's Wisdom
❖ Isn't competition necessary?	❖ Only if balanced by Dharma and Seva.
❖ Can business be cooperative and still grow?	❖ It grows deeper, not just wider.
❖ What's real economic strength?	❖ The ability to rise without pushing others down.

न बुद्धिभेदं जनयेदज्ञानां कर्मसङ्गिनाम् ।
जोषयेत्सर्वकर्माणि विद्वान्युक्त: समाचरन् ॥

na buddhi-bhedaṁ janayed ajñānāṁ karma-saṅginām
joṣhayet sarva-karmāṇi vidvān yuktaḥ samācharan
(Bhagavad Gita, Ch-3, Verse 26)

The wise should not create discord in the intellects of ignorant people, who are attached to fruitive actions, by inducing them to stop work. Rather, by performing their duties in an enlightened manner, they should inspire the ignorant also to do their prescribed duties.

8

Governance: From Greed to Rajarshi: The Vedic Model of Public Leadership

A true leader governs not by decree, but by Dharma.

As the campus erupted into debates about the latest political scandal and budget cuts, Bharat found himself drifting from the noise to a quieter question: Who should rule, and how?

He found Madhav sitting cross-legged under the old banyan tree, leafing through a worn-out copy of the *Mahabharata*.

Professor, Bharat began, we studied public choice theory today. It basically says politicians serve themselves while pretending to serve the people. Is that all governance is, a rigged auction of promises?

Madhav didn't look up. Modern politics runs on the currency of power. Vedic governance ran on the foundation of Dharma.

You mean... ancient kings followed some code?

Not just a code, Madhav replied. They followed consciousness. In the Vedic view, a true ruler is a Rajarshi, a king who is also a sage.

He turned the pages and pointed:

Mahabharata, Shanti Parva:

'The king who governs with Dharma protects the weak, restrains the powerful, and rules for the welfare of all.'

Bharat raised an eyebrow. So instead of campaign slogans, the Vedic ruler read scriptures and listened to sages?

Madhav smiled. And sought inner purification before governing others. The *Bhagavad Gita* puts it clearly, 3.21:

'Whatever a great man does, others follow.'

A Rajarshi doesn't chase votes, he upholds values.

Bharat frowned. Most politicians act like kings but behave like gamblers.

Madhav's tone sharpened. A real king does not gamble with the people's future. Power without Dharma becomes tyranny. Dharma without power becomes helplessness.

Bharat, thinking aloud, began to scribble in his notebook under the heading: Rajarshi vs Modern Politics.

Bharat's Scribble - Comparison Table: Modern Governance vs Vedic Rajarshi Model.

Concept	Modern Politics	Vedic Rajarshi Governance
Goal	Power and popularity	Dharma and public welfare
Method	Lobbying, media, vote banks	Inner discipline, wise counsel, service
Accountability	Electoral cycles	Karmic and moral responsibility
Public Role	Consumer / voter	Family (Kutumba) under king's care

Leadership Ethic	Policy manipulation	Personal sacrifice and justice

So, leadership isn't just policy and polling, it's penance? Bharat asked.

Exactly. Governance is not management, Bharat. It's a sacred duty. A leader must first conquer himself before trying to lead others.

Bharat flipped to a fresh page. Who lived this out? I mean... it sounds poetic, but did any ruler ever actually do it?

Madhav nodded.

King Janaka, renounced yet just, ruled with detachment and wisdom.

Yudhishthira, truthful to a fault, governed not with ambition but with fairness.

Chandragupta, under Chanakya's guidance, combined realpolitik with Dharma.

Bharat added those to his notes, then asked, And in our times?

Look at Nelson Mandela, he led through forgiveness, not vengeance.

Or Gandhi, his Swaraj wasn't about flags, but self-rule rooted in Dharma.

Bharat looked toward the distant administrative building. Seems like we could use a few Rajarshis today.

Madhav closed the *Mahabharata* gently.

We always could. The scriptures weren't written for the past, they were written for the awake.

Key Reflections

Bharat's Curiosity	Madhav's Wisdom
❖ Why do our leaders keep failing us?	❖ Because they forgot that leadership is a burden, not a trophy.
❖ Can Dharma and democracy co-exist?	❖ Only when leaders become servants, not saviors.
❖ So, the Rajarshi wasn't feared but followed?	❖ Followed because he first followed Dharma.

यज्ञदानतप:कर्म न त्याज्यं कार्यमेव तत् |
यज्ञो दानं तपश्चैव पावनानि मनीषिणाम् ||

yajña-dāna-tapaḥ-karma na tyājyaṁ kāryam eva tat
yajño dānaṁ tapaśh chaiva pāvanāni manīṣhiṇām
(Bhagavad Gita, Ch-18, Verse-5)

Actions based upon sacrifice, charity, and penance should never be abandoned; they must certainly be performed. Indeed, acts of sacrifice, charity, and penance are purifying even for those who are wise.

9

Capitalism, Communism, And Consciousness: Transcending Economic Ideologies

When -isms fail, it's time for inner revolution.

The seminar on global ideologies had just wrapped. Inside, students were still hotly debating capitalism versus communism, each defending their - ism like a badge of honour.

Bharat walked out with a cup of tea, visibly weary. He joined Professor Madhav near the neem tree.

Professor, he sighed, capitalism rewards greed, communism crushes aspiration. Is there no third way?

Madhav stirred his tea gently. Yes. It's called consciousness.

Sounds spiritual. But what's the economic model?

None, Madhav replied calmly. That's the beauty of it. It's not about control or systems. It's about awakening.

Bharat frowned. But don't we need policies, frameworks?

You need principles first, Madhav corrected. The Vedas never glorified wealth or poverty. They taught us to align Artha, wealth, with Dharma and Moksha.

He quoted softly:

Isha Upanishad, Verse 1: 'All this is pervaded by the Lord. Enjoy with renunciation. Do not covet.'

Bharat pulled out his notepad and drew a table.

Bharat's Scribble - Comparison Table: Capitalism vs Communism vs Vedantic Economy.

Feature	Capitalism	Communism	Vedantic (Conscious) Economy
Ownership	Private	Collective (State)	Stewardship (Trusteeship

			)
Motivation	Profit	Equality	Dharma and Service (Yajna)
Resource Use	Exploitative	Centralized	Sustainable, Ecological (Rta)
Labor	Commodity	Controlled asset	Duty (Karma Yoga)
Consumption	Maximized	Controlled	Mindful (Aparigraha)
Spiritual Dimension	Ignored	Suppressed	Centered

Capitalism feeds the ego, Bharat said aloud. Communism starves the soul.

Madhav smiled, and consciousness liberates both.

So, what went wrong in the real world? Bharat asked.

Madhav ticked them off gently:

- **Post-2008 Capitalism:** Bailouts for the rich, austerity for the poor.

- **Communist regimes?** Economic stagnation, suppression of thought.
- Even the Scandinavian models, while secular, are closer to a Dharma-driven hybrid: equity, sustainability, and citizen well-being over GDP mania.

Bharat looked up. And what anchors this 'conscious economy' in the Vedas?

Madhav responded without hesitation:

- **Lokasangraha** - Welfare of all.
- **Samatva** - Inner and outer balance.
- **Sarva Loka Hitam** - Benefit of all beings.
- **And the highest: Swaraj** - Not just political freedom, but inner governance.

Professor, Bharat said, reflecting, it feels like we're trying to patch broken ideologies with newer versions of the same virus.

Madhav nodded. Because we design systems to police desire, instead of cultivating people who transcend it.

Key Reflections

Bharat's Curiosity	Madhav's Wisdom
❖ Why do ideologies always disappoint?	❖ Because they treat symptoms, not the soul.
❖ Is there a perfect system?	❖ No. But there can be a conscious society.
❖ So, the future is not post-capitalist or post-communist?	❖ It is post-ego.

अर्जुन उवाच |
नष्टो मोहः स्मृतिर्लब्धा त्वत्प्रसादान्मयाच्युत |
स्थितोऽस्मि गतसन्देहः करिष्ये वचनं तव ||

arjuna uvācha
naṣhṭo mohaḥ smṛitir labdhā tvat-prasādān mayāchyuta
sthito 'smi gata-sandehaḥ kariṣhye vachanaṁ tava
(Bhagavad Gita, Ch-18, Verse-73)

Arjun said: O Infallible One, by Your grace my illusion has been dispelled, and I am situated in knowledge. I am now free from doubts, and I shall act according to Your instructions.

10

The Vedantonomics Upanishad: A Manifesto for The Future

When wisdom transcends models,
a new scripture begins.

The monsoon clouds were heavy, and so was Bharat's mind. He had walked with theories, laughed with logic, and meditated on markets. But something still stirred in him, an urge to give this journey a form, a legacy.

Professor, he said, pausing under the rustle of a neem tree near the faculty block, if what we've uncovered is truly transformative, shouldn't we document it, not just as a book, but as a new Upanishad?

Madhav's eyes twinkled.

Ah! The Vedantonomics Upanishad. Now that sounds like a scripture worth reading... and writing.

But I'm no rishi, Bharat laughed. Just a recovering economist.

Exactly, Madhav smiled. That makes you perfect for it. This time, the sage wears a blazer and carries a chai thermos.

A Glimpse into the Vedantonomics Upanishad

The economist who sees beyond models, and the sage who sees within markets, are one in realization.

Madhav: You must start with the fundamentals. Not of supply and demand, but of Dharma.

The Vedantic Equation of Purpose

Ph = f (Dh, Ar, Ka, Mo)

Bharat (grinning): So, this is the GDP of the soul?

Madhav: Precisely. It's the formula for Puruṣārtha, the goal of human life. Where Artha fuels, Kama energizes, Dharma guides, and Moksha liberates.

Bharat: Growth with a GPS. That's Vedantonomics.

How Desires are Born: The Gunas Behind the Demand Curve

Ka = f (SG, RG, TG)

Madhav: Sattva births clarity. Rajas, ambition. Tamas, chaos. The quality of our desires shapes the destiny of our economies.

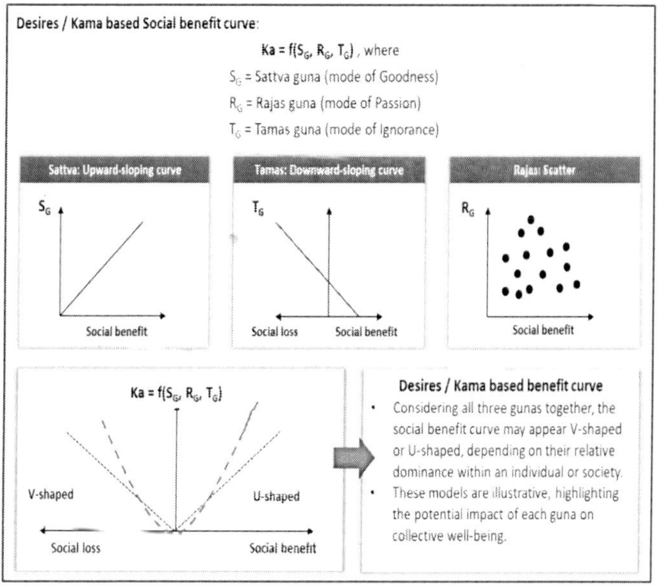

Bharat: So, we now have behavioural economics... with Sanskrit footnotes.

Madhav: Modern economics grew tall but hollow. Rational man. Efficient markets. Infinite wants. All assumptions, never soul-searched.

Bharat: So much GDP, yet so little grace.

Madhav: And where did it lead us? To the 2008 subprime crisis, where imaginary wealth collapsed like a sandcastle in a storm. All that brilliant financial engineering, CDOs, credit default swaps, leverage ratios, and yet, it couldn't detect a simple truth: greed is unstable.

Bharat: And governments? They bailed out banks, not people.

Madhav: Dharma was absent. Artha ruled. And Kama, unchecked, brought us to the brink.

Bharat: And again, in the pandemic. Fiscal stimulus packages flowed, but distribution failed. The poorest walked miles home while stock markets hit all-time highs.

Madhav: When Artha loses its moral compass, inequality is not just an outcome, it becomes a policy.

Bharat: And now geopolitics looks like a battlefield of egos.

Madhav (sighing): The current world order is intoxicated by Rajas and blinded by Tamas. Powerful nations act like traders in destruction, profiting from the wars they help ignite, selling weapons while preaching peace.

Bharat: They call themselves 'superpowers' but act like super-profiteers.

Madhav: And they feed the war-mongers. Cartels disguised as allies, sanctions masquerading as virtue. Meanwhile, millions starve. The Dharma of diplomacy has vanished.

Bharat: Instead of ***Vasudhaiva Kutumbakam***, we now have **'*Vasudhaiva Vibhajanam*'**, the world divided for profit.

Madhav: Which is why Vedantonomics matters. It restores cosmic order, Rta, where peace is not a strategy, but a shared responsibility.

Core Principles of Vedantonomics:

1. **Dharma** - Centric Economy
2. **Beyond GDP** - Redefining Progress
3. Sustainable Living - Aparigraha, Rta
4. Ethical Entrepreneurship - Yajna, Karma Yoga
5. **Stewardship Mindset** - Ishavasya Idam Sarvam
6. Education for Wholeness
7. **Global Family Ethos** - Vasudhaiva Kutumbakam
8. Inner Development as True Wealth

Challenges & Implementation

- **Paradigm Shift:** From ego to eco.
- **Measurement Gaps:** Dharma doesn't fit spreadsheets.
- **Inertia:** Systems protect comfort zones.
- **Practicality:** Wisdom must walk in policy corridors.

Steps Forward:

- Local pilots, ethical curricula, values-led policy, conscious capitalism.

Bharat: What about Diminishing marginal utility. Even my favourite chocolate feels less divine after the fifth bite.

Madhav: Gita said it first. 'Pleasures born of senses begin like nectar, end as poison.' (Gita 18.38)

Bharat: So even Alfred Marshall was a closet Vedantin?

Madhav: Perhaps. But Vedanta goes beyond just noticing the decline. It explains *why* it happens, and how to transcend it (MU).

Bharat: Do tell, Professor! I've been seeking spiritual insight between spoonfuls of ice cream.

Madhav (laughing): In Vedantic thought, desires are like Rakta Beej, the demon who multiplies every time you strike him. Fulfill one, and five more arise. The Gita warns:

'Attachment breeds desire, desire breeds anger, and anger leads to delusion.' (2.62)

Bharat: So, desires aren't just insatiable. They're downright demonic!

Madhav: Unless tamed with Santosha (contentment) and Aparigraha (non-hoarding). Vedanta doesn't reject pleasure; it tells you which pleasure is sustainable. The joy of a good action is better than a gluttonous binge.

Bharat: This explains the economics of why my third samosa was regrettable, morally and gastronomically.

Madhav: Exactly! And look at today's world, tech giants chasing your eyeballs, investment banks stacking billions on leveraged promises, stock market bubbles growing fatter on digital dreams. The marginal utility of wealth and power? Diminishing. And yet, they consume more, driven by Rajas and wrapped in Tamas.

Bharat: Even some regulators have become Rakta Beej allies, turning a blind eye as corruption flourishes like a hedge fund in heat.

Madhav: Because when Dharma is outsourced to compliance checklists, ethics become loopholes.

Bharat: So DMU isn't just a demand curve. It's a warning label.

Madhav: Indeed. A spiritual compass, pointing not to more, but to enough.

Bharat: Where Marshall meets Maharishi. And Warren Buffett finally shakes hands with Yudhishthira.

Bharat: This isn't a book anymore. It's a scripture. A movement.

Madhav: Then let it be lived. The real economy starts when the soul stops outsourcing its purpose.

Bharat: I'll write the *Vedantonomics Upanishad.* With verses, commentary... maybe even charts!

Madhav: And I'll bless it, with footnotes and foot-wisdom.

They both laughed.

Thus ends the penultimate teaching of Vedantonomics. The final one lies in silence.

11

The Final Question: Who Is the Economist, really?

The last question is not what you earn or buy, but who you are becoming.

The semester was closing like a well-written thesis, structured, intense, but leaving behind the faint scent of an unfinished idea.

Under the old banyan tree, Bharat and Madhav sat with their familiar clay cups of chai. The breeze smelled of impending rain, and the soil had that wet, philosophical aroma.

Bharat: Professor, we've travelled from GDP to Gita, from demand curves to Dharma but one question lingers. Who is the economist, really?

Madhav (smiling): Define 'economist.' The one who models rational agents on spreadsheets? Or the one who calculates the karmic ROI of every action?

Bharat smirked: Both. And neither. Maybe the true economist is the one who understands the invisible balance sheet, the karma ledger, the Dharma dashboard, and the Moksha forecast.

Madhav: Now that... sounds like someone who's ready to write a new kind of textbook.

They slipped quietly.

Bharat: Do you think the world is ready for Vedantonomics?

Madhav: Was the world ever ready for the Gita at Kurukshetra? *Truth arrives when the battlefield is noisy!*

Bharat: And this battlefield is... loud. War economies thrive, greed wears a necktie, and GDP rises as the forests fall.

Madhav: Because most economists are counting coins while the soul bleeds. Look at today, defence spending balloons while education starves. Markets cheer layoffs. And social media algorithms hijack free will.

Bharat: They've turned desire into a subscription model. Even detachment now comes with a promo code.

Madhav (laughing): Exactly. But the true economist, my friend, measures not price but peace. Not output but outgrowth.

Bharat: So then, the real economist... is part Yudhishthira, part Keynes, part Kabir.

Madhav: And wholly awake.

A soft gust swept through the banyan leaves.

Bharat nodded slowly: So, this is not the end of our dialogue?

Madhav (chuckling): We've just scratched the surface. Economics, like life, is a deep ocean. We've only dipped our toes. There's still the whole Mahabharata of market psychology, the Upanishads of sustainable models, and don't get me started on yogic taxation principles.

Bharat (laughing): Yogic taxation?

Madhav: Of course!

First tax your ego, then rebate your attachments, and finally declare Moksha as your net income.

They both burst out laughing.

Just then, a voice from behind startled them.

John (hesitantly): Excuse me... I hope I'm not intruding. I've overheard bits of your conversation over the past week while passing by. I'm John, a visiting student from the US under the international collaboration program. I study economics too, but...

this is different. This is deeper. Could I... maybe learn from you?

Bharat and Madhav turned.

John looked nervous, but earnest. A spark of the same curiosity that once lit Bharat's eyes flickered in John's.

Madhav (smiling knowingly): Ah. The ripple begins.

He looked at Bharat.

Madhav: Your first student, Professor Bharat.

Bharat (surprised): Wait, me?

Madhav (grinning): Of course. You've graduated from questions to stewardship. It's time to build the future with this wisdom. Teach him not just models, but meaning.

John: Is there... a textbook for this?

Bharat (laughing): No textbook yet. But a lot of tea, a banyan tree, and questions. That's how it starts.

Madhav: And when in doubt, remember the three pillars of Yogic Economics: tax your ego, rebate your attachments, and file your intentions with the Divine Revenue Service.

They all laughed.

Then, with a calm smile, Madhav stood up and said, Let's meet again soon. Maybe under a different tree. In another city. Perhaps in a society that finally values wisdom over wealth.

Bharat: And until then?

Madhav: Contemplate. Question. Share. Start the ripple.

They stood up.

Bharat touched his professor's feet. I'm no longer afraid of economic contradictions. I'm curious about the soul's equations.

Madhav placed his hand gently on Bharat's head.

Good. Then go be an economist, not of models, but of meaning.

As Madhav turned and slowly walked into the misty tree-lined path, a golden glint appeared behind the clouds. For a fleeting moment, Bharat felt he wasn't just saying goodbye to a teacher, but to something cosmic. Something eternal.

And beside him now stood John, wide-eyed, eager, and ready to walk the same path.

They both stood silently for a moment, gazing in the direction where Madhav had disappeared.

John (breaking the silence): Was he always like that? Like a walking Veda with a wi-fi connection to the cosmos?

Bharat (smiling): He's not a professor. He's a phenomenon. And yes, sometimes I still wonder if he even aged.

John: So, what now? Are there Vedantonomics classes, or do I need to apply to the School of Existential Chill?

Bharat (laughing): Well, the enrolment criteria are strict: unlearn what you know, question everything, drink lots of chai, and get used to cosmic sarcasm.

John: You're serious?

Bharat: About the chai? Deadly serious. But John... this isn't a course. It's a revolution dressed as a conversation.

John: Is there a syllabus?

Bharat: Only one rule: every answer must lead to a deeper question. That's how you know you're getting close.

They both turned back to the banyan tree. The breeze felt different now. As if the roots had heard everything.

John (grinning): Do you think Madhav will come back?

Bharat: I don't know. But somehow... I feel like he never really left.

John: And this ripple... it's real, isn't it?

Bharat: Very real. And you just became wave number two.

They walked away slowly, but the echo of their laughter and questions lingered like incense in the air.

Somewhere in the sky, a crow cawed.

Somewhere in a boardroom, a soul sighed.

And somewhere in the unseen pages of time, the next chapter of Vedantonomics quietly began.

Final Reflections

Question	Vedantic Response
❖ Who is the real economist?	❖ The one who aligns Artha with Dharma and seeks Moksha over models.
❖ What is true wealth?	❖ Inner peace, contentment (Santosha), and the ability to act selflessly.
❖ What is development?	❖ Not rising GDP but rising consciousness.
❖ What is the role of policy?	❖ To uphold Dharma, reduce suffering, and foster harmony.

If you want to be rich, count your contributions, not your currency.

- Professor Madhav

If you want to lead, master your desires first.

- Bharat

इति ते ज्ञानमाख्यातं गुह्याद्गुह्यतरं मया |
विमृश्यैतदशेषेण यथेच्छसि तथा कुरु || 63||

iti te jñānam ākhyātaṁ guhyād guhyataraṁ mayā
vimṛiśhyaitad aśheṣheṇa yathechchhasi tathā kuru
(Bhagavad Gita, Ch-18, Verse-63)

Thus, I have explained to you this knowledge that is more secret than all secrets. Ponder over it deeply, and then do as you wish.

Whispers Beneath the Banyan: Chai, Charts, And Consciousness

By the banks of thought, where Dharma flows...

Beneath the banyan, where chai cups clink,
A tale was told, not in ink-
But in silence, jokes, and sacred debate,
Of how Artha bows when Dharma's great.

Bharat arrived with a capitalist frown,
Armed with models to weigh the town.
Rational man, he declared with flair,
Until life proved irrational everywhere.

Why, he asked, with so many charts?
Do nations fail and break their hearts?
Is greed the gear of global design?
Or have we priced the soul out of line?

Madhav smiled with eyes like dawn,
His words, half shloka, half quiet yawn.
He spoke of Gita, of Karma's net,
Of balance sheets we haven't met.

Desire, he warned, is Rakta Beej.
Each one you feed breeds another siege.
So, tax your ego, rebate your greed,
Declare Moksha as your ultimate need.

They laughed at Keynes, toasted Kabir,
Predicted bubbles over cups of cheer.
They saw through crises, through debt and war,
That every profit leaves a karmic scar.

The stock exchange shook with every verse,
As GDP wept in an ethical hearse.
And while the world raced for quarterly fame,
They asked: Who is the self behind the name?

Then came John, from a Western shore,
With curiosity knocking at Dharma's door.
Is this Economics? Or divine satire?
Both, said Bharat, and something higher.

There's no syllabus, just open skies,
No exams, just soulful whys.
No degree, just Vedantic grace,
To lead not markets, but the human race.

So, if you ever question your pay,
Or if your growth has lost its way,
Remember the banyan, the chai, the breeze,
Where wisdom whispered through rustling leaves.

अथातो ब्रह्मजिज्ञासा ।

Athato brahma jijnasa

(Vedanta Sutras, Aphorism-1)

Now, therefore, inquiry into Brahman

the commencement of an investigation into the nature of ultimate reality!!

A Whisper to The Reader

Dear reader,

You've walked through the forest of Vedantonomics, a place where economists chant shlokas and sages solve market failures. But this is not the end. Like any good Upanishad, the silence after the story says more than the story itself.

There are questions we haven't asked. Dialogues yet to happen. May be next time we will dive deeper.

Until then, reflect. Reconsider. Rewrite your own economic story.

And when the winds of curiosity rise again, you'll hear it, under some tree, in some part of the world:

Professor, I have another question.

And I have another cup of tea.

Stay tuned. Or better yet, stay wise.

Genesis of Thought

Integrating Vedic Philosophy with Modern Economic Principle

For the roots to nourish, they must be remembered.

Long before numbers ruled nations, and policies were shaped in spreadsheets, a different economics guided civilization. One where the currency was character, wealth was wedded to wisdom, and the economy was not an industry, but an extension of ecology and ethics. That economics had no Wall Street. Its spine was *Dharma*, and its heartbeat, *Satya* (truth).

Vedantonomics is not an invention. It is a *recollection*. It is the remembering of a framework that once governed empires without enslaving people. A framework where the means mattered as much as the ends, where production was inseparable from purpose, and where consumption was balanced by *contentment*, not credit cards.

The genesis of this thought was born from a personal conflict.

As a student of modern economics, I (Amit) often found myself disenchanted. The assumptions of rational self-interest, infinite wants, perfect markets, seemed elegant on paper but hollow in life. The models explained the 'how' but not the 'why'. I witnessed recessions that graphs couldn't prevent, inequality that theories couldn't justify, and environmental degradation that growth statistics chose to ignore.

But deep within, there echoed the voice of an older logic, whispers from my Vedic heritage. And those whispers became a roar when Bharat, my alter ego, met Professor Madhav.

It is in their dialogue that this philosophical journey begins.

The Philosophical Framing: Beyond Dualities

At its core, Vedantonomics is a conversation between the material and the spiritual. It does not reject economics, it refines it. It does not romanticize poverty, it redefines prosperity.

The philosophical pillars of Vedantonomics arise from four Vedic goals of human life:

- **Dharma** - the compass of ethics, duty, social harmony.
- **Artha** - the rightful acquisition and use of resources.
- **Kāma** - the pursuit of joy and desires in balance.
- **Mokṣa** - liberation, self-realization, and freedom from cycles.

Together, these form the **Chaturvidha Purushartha**, a holistic architecture of fulfilment. Vedantonomics uses these as the new coordinates for defining growth and value.

The Contrasts It Seeks to Heal

Modern Economics	Vedantonomics
Self-interest as foundation	Self-awareness as foundation
Infinite wants	Wise restraint
Utility maximization	Dharma-aligned purpose maximization
External incentives	Inner motivation (Svabhava-driven)

GDP-centric growth	Holistic human flourishing
Scarcity mindset	Abundance through balance

Vedantic Sources that Frame This Work

- **Bhagavad Gita:** For insights on *Karma Yoga*, *Swadharma*, detachment, and righteous action.
- **Upanishads:** For the metaphysical framing of human potential and interconnectedness.
- **Manusmṛiti:** For socio-economic order, duties, justice, and moral law.
- **Arthaśāstra:** For pragmatic statecraft and ancient models of sustainable economic governance.
- **Mahābhārata:** As epics illustrating the economic, ethical, and ecological consequences of adharma.

These texts are not dogma here, they are design logic. They are used not as scriptures, but as structural blueprints to shape a more sustainable, ethical, and inclusive economic architecture.

A Living Philosophy

Vedantonomics is not a return to the past. It is a rebirth of the perennial. It speaks to artificial intelligence, crypto economies, market meltdowns, and climate chaos. But it speaks *through* the lens of inner intelligence, *viveka*, and not just data analytics.

Through the dialogues between Bharat and Professor Madhav in this book, you were not given formulas to memorize, but questions to contemplate. You were invited to think deeply, to unlearn assumptions, and to perceive the market not as a mechanical system, but as a mirror reflecting human consciousness.

And if, by the end, you feel a quiet discomfort, that the world needs more than new policies, it needs older wisdom, then the genesis is complete.

Key Concepts from Economics & Vedanta

Economics Terms

- **Capitalism** - An economic system based on private property, market freedom, and profit maximization.
- **Communism** - A system advocating collective ownership, state control, and equitable distribution.
- **GDP (Gross Domestic Product)** - The total value of goods and services produced in a country within a specific timeframe.
- **Invisible Hand** - Adam Smith's metaphor for how individual self-interest can lead to societal good.
- **Utility** - The satisfaction or benefit derived from a good or service.
- **Market Failure** - A situation where free markets do not allocate resources efficiently or justly.

- **Externalities** - Side effects (positive or negative) of economic actions on third parties.
- **Rational Choice Theory** - Assumes individuals make decisions to maximize utility based on preferences and constraints.
- **Fiscal Policy** - Government's use of spending and taxation to influence the economy.
- **Consumerism** - The ideology that promotes the acquisition of goods and services in ever-increasing amounts.

Vedic Terms

- **Vedanta** - A school of Hindu philosophy based on the Upanishads, focusing on self realization and the unity of all existence.
- **Dharma** - Righteous duty; the moral and ethical path aligned with cosmic law.
- **Karma** - The universal law of cause and effect; every action has consequences across time.
- **Moksha** - Liberation; freedom from the cycle of birth and death.
- **Artha** - The pursuit of material prosperity and resources.

- **Kama** - Desire; the pursuit of pleasure in alignment with Dharma.
- **Yajna** - A sacred offering or sacrifice, symbolizing collaboration and shared welfare.
- **Sattva / Rajas / Tamas** - The three gunas or modes of material nature: clarity, passion, and ignorance.
- **Aparigraha** - Non-possessiveness; the principle of minimalism and detachment from accumulation.
- **Seva** - Selfless service done without expectation of reward.
- **Samatva** - Equanimity; treating pleasure and pain, success and failure, with evenness of mind.
- **Rajarshi** - A ruler who is also a sage; governance guided by inner wisdom.
- **Swaraj** - Self-rule, both political independence and inner mastery; freedom rooted in discipline.
- **Lokasangraha** - Welfare of all; the collective upliftment of society.
- **Sarva Loka Hitam** - That which benefits all beings.